For Lindsey and Kathryn, with much love and gratitude · VF

© 2006 The Chicken House

First published in the United Kingdom in 2006 by
The Chicken House, 2 Palmer Street, Frome,
Somerset, BA11 1DS
www.doublecluck.com

Text © 2006 Vivian French
Illustrations © 2006 AnnaLaura Cantone, Ross Collins,
Joelle Dreidemy, Andrea Huseinovic
Cover © 2006 Ross Collins

Designed by Ian Butterworth

Printed and bound in China for Imago

British Library Cataloguing in Publication
Data available
Library of Congress Cataloguing in Publication
data available

ISBN: 1 904442 57 9

THE Daddy Goose COLLECTION

As told to Vivian French

Illustrated by

AnnaLaura Cantone, Ross Collins,
Joelle Dreidemy, Andrea Huseinovic

Chicken House

2 Palmer Street, Frome,
Somerset BA11 1DS

Meet Daddy Goose!

For hundreds of years little children have heard

About Old Mother Goose, a remarkable bird

Whose pockets and baskets are stuffed full of rhyme –

But now is the moment, and now is the time

For a WHOOSH! for a ZOOM! and the SPARKLE! of stars

As Daddy Goose circles round Venus and Mars

Then dives with a VROOM! and a WHIZZ! and a FIZZ!

Is he coming to see us? He is! Yes, he is!

He's bringing us stories of Hey Diddle Diddle

(To tell us just WHY Puss was playing a fiddle,)

The tale of a clock, and of merry King Cole,

And little Miss Muffet, with curds in a bowl.

There's Humpty, and Mary, there's Jack and there's Jill

And where is the Black Sheep? Why, up on the hill!

For Old Mother Goose may have rhymes we know well

But it's DADDY who knows all the stories to tell!

So pick up this book, and cuddle up tight,
And let Daddy Goose tell your story tonight. . . .

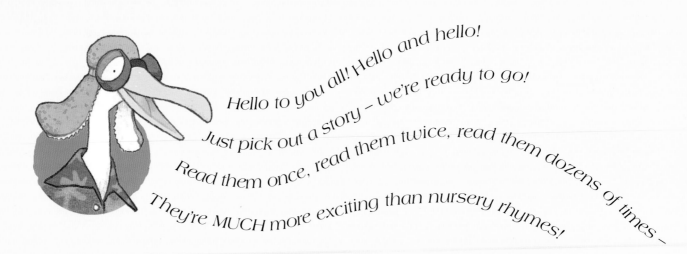

Hello to you all! Hello and hello!

Just pick out a story – we're ready to go!

Read them once, read them twice, read them dozens of times –

They're MUCH more exciting than nursery rhymes!

Contents

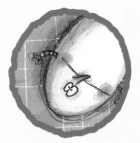

Hey Diddle Diddle

Hey diddle diddle,
The cat and the fiddle,
The cow jumped over the moon;
The little dog laughed
To see such sport,
And the dish ran away with the spoon.

When Lilly the cow was little, she didn't like living in a field and eating grass. Not at all. Not one bit. She wanted to hop and skip and jump, and be Very Famous Indeed. Her Mam said, 'Don't be silly, Lilly. Cows are never famous.' Lilly didn't agree.

One evening, when her Mam was dozing, Lilly ran away. She hopped and she skipped and she ran, and she jumped right out of the field. Right into town Lilly ran, and there she stopped. The town was very busy. Shopkeepers were shutting up their shops with a clatter. Men and women were hurrying home from work. Children were running home for their tea. Lilly stood and stared.

WOOF!'

Lilly looked down and saw a little dog. On his arm was a basket, and inside was a grumpy-looking tin dish and an angry-looking silver spoon.

'Hello,' said the dog. 'What's your name?'

'Lilly,' said Lilly.

The little dog laughed. 'My name's Billy,' he said. 'Billy and Lilly! We'd better stick together.'

'All right,' said Lilly. 'But I've come to town because I want to be a Very Famous Cow.'

'Well I never,' said Billy. 'I'm trying to be a Very Famous Juggler, but I'm not very good at it yet.' And he threw the dish and the spoon high in the air, but then –TINKLE! TINKLE! CRASH!!!

'OW! OW! OW!' moaned the dish.

'OW! OW! OW!' groaned the spoon. The noise made Lilly jump. She jumped so high, she jumped up through a window and into a house.

'MEEOW!'

Lilly looked, and saw a cat sitting on a sofa.

'Hello,' said the cat. 'What's your name?'

'Lilly,' said Lilly.

'Meeow!' mewed the cat. 'My name's Milly. Milly and Lilly! We'd better be friends.'

'All right,' said Lilly. 'But I've come to town because I want to be a Very Famous Cow.'

'Fancy that,' said Milly. 'I'm trying to be a Very Famous Musician.' She picked up a fiddle and began to play.

SCREECH! SCREECH! SCREECH!

The screeching was so loud that Lilly jumped straight back out of the window.

Billy was waiting down below. 'That's clever,' he said. 'I didn't know cows could jump.'

'I can,' said Lilly.

'How high can you jump?' Billy asked. 'As high as I throw my dish and my spoon?'

Lilly was feeling proud of herself. She looked up at the stars in the dark night sky. 'As high as the moon,' she said.

'Nobody could jump as high as that,' said Billy.

'I can,' said Lilly. 'Just watch!'

But when Lilly tried to jump as high as the moon she ended up on a roof instead. Milly was sitting on a chimney pot. 'Meeow!' she mewed in surprise. 'What are you doing here?'

'I was trying to jump as high as the moon,' Lilly said sadly. 'But I couldn't jump high enough.'

'Let me play you a jumping tune,' said Milly, and she began to play her fiddle.

SCREECH! SCREECH! SCRATCHITTY! SCRATCHITTY!

'Moo!' said Lilly. 'MOO!' and before she knew it she was jumping up and up and up . . . right over the moon. Down in the street below, men and women and children stared and stared and stared.

'LOOK!' they said to each other. 'Look! A cow jumping over the moon! Whoever heard of a cow that could jump so high!' Billy the dog laughed and laughed. He was laughing so much he didn't see the tin dish pick itself up from the ground.

'All I want is a quiet life,' it grumbled.

'Me too,' said the silver spoon. They looked at each other, shook hands . . . and ran away.

Nobody noticed them going. They were all much too busy cheering the cow who had jumped right over the moon.

'She'll be a Very Famous Cow now,' said Billy.

'She certainly will,' said Milly. 'Do you know, Billy – I think I might try jumping instead of music.'

'I was thinking of jumping instead of juggling, too,' said Billy.

'Let's practise together!' said Milly.

'Hurrah!' said Billy.

'Hurrah!' said Billy.

Little Miss Muffet

Little Miss Muffet
Sat on a tuffet
Eating her curds and whey;
There came a big spider,
Who sat down beside her,
And frightened Miss Muffet away!

Speeder Spider was fed up. No one *ever* wanted to play with him. Every time anyone saw him they shouted, 'UGH!!!! It's a great big horrible hairy spider!' and ran away.

He found Little Boy Blue asleep under the haystack. When Speeder tickled his nose to wake him up, Little Boy Blue said, 'OOOF! Go away!'

He heard Little Bo Peep calling for her sheep in the orchard where he lived.

'Sheepie sheep!' she called. 'Where are you?'

'Cooeee!' said Speeder hopefully, 'Cooeee!' But Little Bo Peep ran off calling, 'Sheepie! Wait for me!' When Speeder saw Jack and Jill he didn't bother to follow them.

'They've got each other to play with,' he said sadly.

Not long after that Speeder saw a little girl walking towards the orchard carrying a blue china bowl. A bigger girl walked behind her carrying a three-legged stool. Speeder ran along a branch of the cherry tree to have a better look.

'Here you are, Molly Muffet,' said the big girl, and she put the stool under Speeder's tree. 'You sit here.'

'Won't you stay, Tess?' Molly asked. 'It's so lovely under the trees.'

Tess shuddered. 'There might be great big horrible hairy spiders! Now, eat your supper.'

'But I don't like curds and whey,' Molly Muffet said. 'It's all lumpy and slimy and horrible and DISGUSTING.'

Tess shook her head. 'You must eat it, Molly, or Mother will be mad.' And she left Molly sitting on her little stool staring gloomily at her supper.

Speeder peered out from under the leaves.

'Little Miss Muffet!' he called. 'Little Miss Muffet! Would you like cherries instead?' And he dropped a shiny red cherry onto the grass. Molly picked it up. 'Thank you!' she said. She looked up into the tree to see who was talking to her, but all she could see was leaves. 'I LOVE cherries. But Mother will be cross if I don't eat my disgusting, horrible, lumpy, slimy, curds and whey.'

'Couldn't you spill it by-mistake-on-purpose?' Speeder suggested.

Molly licked her spoon thoughtfully. 'I think Mother would guess. She's very clever at guessing things like that.'

'Suppose you had a horrid fright?' Speeder said. 'Suppose a great big horrible hairy spider came and frightened you?'

'But I'm not frightened of spiders,' Molly said. 'Tess hates them, but I like them.'

Speeder's heart went pit-a-pit-pat with excitement. 'Could you *pretend* to be frightened?' he asked.

'Oh, YES,' said Molly.

'Then here's the plan!' said Speeder. 'I'll come and sit down beside you. You scream and drop your bowl - and everyone will think it's because you're scared!'

Molly stared up into the cherry tree. '*Are* you a SPIDER? Hurrah! I've always wanted a spider as a friend. Come out and say hello!'

'Molly! Molly Muffet!' It was Molly's sister calling from the garden. 'Have you eaten your supper?'

'QUICK!' Speeder whispered. 'Get ready!'

'I've nearly finished,' Molly called back.

Just as Tess reached the trees, Speeder sailed down on his silver thread — and sat on the stool beside Molly.

'Oh! Oh! Oh!' shouted Molly, and she jumped up, tumbled her bowl into the grass, and ran away to her sister.

'OH! OH! OH!' screamed Tess. 'It's a great big horrible hairy spider!' and she grabbed Molly's hand and rushed her home.

Speeder whizzed up his thread and into his tree to wait. It wasn't long before Molly came running back.

'That was FUN,' she said, her eyes shining. 'And look! I've got a plate of bread and strawberry jam! Come and share it.'

So Molly and Speeder shared the bread and jam and cherries . . . and giggled about what might happen if ever Tess found Speeder in *her* bowl of curds and whey!

ROUND AND ROUND THE GARDEN

Round and round the garden
Like a teddy bear;
One step, two step,
Tickle you under there!

Freddie and Flora were twins, and one birthday Gran gave them each a teddy bear. Freddie loved his Big Ted, and took him wherever he went. At night Big Ted slept on his pillow. Flora loved her Fluffy Ted, but she often left him under the bed, or in the kitchen, or in the bathroom. Fluffy Ted never knew WHERE he was going to spend the night. . . .

One day Flora took Fluffy Ted out into the garden, and forgot to bring him in.

That night Big Ted did his best to show Flora that something was wrong. He wouldn't sit up when Mum put him on a chair to watch the twins having their tea. He flopped over when Dad was reading a bedtime story. He even slithered off Freddie's pillow onto the floor, but it was no good. Dad put him back, and no one noticed that Fluffy Ted was missing.

'I'll have to go and find him when the twins are asleep,' Big Ted decided, and he tried not to feel scared.

24

Big Ted waited until the house was quiet, and then slid out of bed. His heart was beating fast as he tiptoed onto the landing, and every noise made him jump.

'The quicker I go, the sooner I'll be safely back in bed,' he told himself as he crept down the stairs. He was hurrying towards the back door when –

CRASH!!! – Spotty Cat came bouncing through the cat flap.

'Meeow!' said Spotty. 'What are YOU doing here?'

'I'm going to fetch Fluffy Ted,' said Big Ted, as bravely as he could. 'Flora left him in the garden. Er . . . is it VERY dark out there?'

'Black as pitch!' Spotty said. 'Shall I hold the cat flap open for you?'

'Oh, yes PLEASE,' Big Ted said, and he wriggled his way out.

'Don't get any fatter, or you'll get stuck!' Spotty said. 'See you later!' And she let the flap drop down behind Big Ted with a

snap!

Big Ted stood outside the back door, and stared into the darkness. He could hear strange little squeaks and creaks. EEEEEK!!! CREAK!!! He could hear rustlings and rattlings. RUSTLE RUSTLE . . .

RATTLE RATTLE . . . He could hear tappings and patterings. TAP TAP . . .

PITTER PATTER . . .

Big Ted swallowed hard, and stepped out onto the grass.

'Fluffy Ted!' he whispered in a wobbly voice. 'Fluffy Ted! Where are you? I've come to fetch you home!'

HOOOT! HOOOOOOOT!

An owl flip-flapped over the garden.

'Oh dear,' Big Ted said to himself. 'I do so wish I was back in my lovely cosy bed, all cuddled up beside Freddie! I'll call once more, and if there's still no answer I'll go home.'

Big Ted crept further into the garden, and took a deep breath.

'FLUFFY TED!' he called, 'ARE YOU THERE?'

Pit pat, pit pat. Pit pat, pit pat . . . what was that behind him? Big Ted froze.

He slowly turned around, and –

JUMPED!

Something soft and tickly was under his nose. ATCHOOO!
He couldn't help sneezing.

'BIG TED!' cried Fluffy Ted. 'It's ME!'

'Oh, Fluffy Ted!' gasped Big Ted. 'I thought you'd be scared out
here by yourself! Instead YOU scared ME!'

'But I WAS scared, Big Ted,' said Fluffy Ted. 'I've been round and
ROUND the garden. It was so dark I couldn't find the door. Then I
heard Tabby talking to you, and I thought, HURRAH! for Big Ted. I
came one step, two steps, and there I was – TICKLING YOUR NOSE!
But I didn't mean to scare you!' And Fluffy Ted gave Big Ted a great
big bear hug. 'I'm SO pleased to see you.'

'Come on,' said Big Ted happily, 'let's go home.'

So Big Ted and Fluffy Ted scrambled back through the cat flap,
and climbed up the stairs back to
the twins' bedroom. When
Flora woke up in the
morning she was
VERY surprised
to see Big Ted
and Fluffy Ted
cuddled up
together on
Freddie's
pillow.

'HEY!' she
said. 'That's
MY bear!' And
she gave Fluffy
Ted a loving
squeeze, and
tucked him under
her duvet.

29

OLD KING COLE

Old King Cole
Was a merry old soul,
And a merry old soul was he;
He called for his pipe,
And he called for his bowl,
And he called for his fiddlers three.

Old King Cole was cross. He'd lost his pipe, and he couldn't find it anywhere. He asked the queen, but she said she hadn't seen it. 'Smoking is BAD for you,' she said.

Old King Cole asked the Prime Minister, but he didn't know where the pipe was. Nor did the three little princes.

'Oh, RHUBARB!' said Old King Cole. 'It's so soothing to blow a smoke ring or two.'

As the days went by, Old King Cole gave up smiling. He never laughed. When the three fiddlers came to play he sat and groaned.

'What's the matter with Grandpa?' asked Prince Tom.

'He's missing his pipe,' said Prince Jim.

'Well,' said Prince Tom, 'I think we should find him a new one. Where do you buy pipes?'

'I don't know,' said Prince Danny. 'Let's ask the Prime Minister.'

'He's too grand to talk to us,' said Prince Jim. 'Let's ask the boy who cleans the boots.'

The boot boy smiled when the princes asked him about pipes.

'My Great Uncle Angus loves pipes,' he said. 'He's got lots. Shall I ask him to come to the palace?'

'Oh, yes PLEASE!' said Prince Danny.

'It'll be a wonderful surprise for Grandpa!' said Prince Tom.

'Could you ask him to come this evening?' asked Prince Jim.

'OK,' said the boot boy, and he hurried away.

The afternoon went far too slowly for the three princes. Old King Cole sat and grumbled. When the queen offered him a cup of tea he told her to GO AWAY. The queen burst into tears and ran out of the room.

'Don't cry, Grandma,' said Prince Tom.

'We're going to surprise him this evening!' said Prince Jim.

Prince Danny whispered, 'We've got him lots of NEW pipes!'

'But smoking is BAD for him,' sobbed the queen. 'I threw his pipe away . . . I never thought it would make him so grumpy!'

'He'll be all right tonight,' Prince Tom said. 'Just wait and see!' The queen wiped her eyes. 'Maybe it IS a good idea to let him have his pipe back,' she said. 'I can't bear him being so miserable.'

The evening came at last. The fiddlers came marching in to play their fiddles, and the three princes began to look hopefully at the door.

'Tonight,' said the first fiddler, 'we have a special tune for Your Majesty!'

EEeeeeeeeeeeeeEEEEEEeeeeeeeeeeEEEEEEEEeeeeeeeeeEEEEEeee!!!

The wailing noise made even Old King Cole sit up. The queen's eyes opened wide, and the princes hid behind the throne.

EEeeeeeeeeeeeeeEEEEEEeeeeeeeeeeEEEEEEEeeeeeeeeeeeeEEEEEEeeee!!!!!

The door opened, and in strode the boot boy's Great Uncle Angus . . . playing the bagpipes.

'I'm here with the pipes, Your Majesty,' said Great Uncle Angus, and he began to play a rollicking tune.

The fiddles joined in. The Princes snapped their fingers, and Old King Cole leapt up from his throne.

'Hurrah!' he shouted, and he seized the queen and whirled her round and round.

Faster went the pipes. Faster went the fiddles. Faster went Old King Cole . . . until at last the music stopped.

'Phew!' said Old King Cole as he wiped his forehead. 'That was GRAND! Piper! I shall be calling for you every evening!' Great Uncle Angus bowed.

'And . . . would you teach me how to play?' Great Uncle Angus bowed again, and Old King Cole picked up the bagpipes.

AAAAAAAAAAAaaaaaaaaAAAAAAAAAAAAAaaaaaaaaaAAAAAAAAAAAAaaaaaaaoooooiiiiYowiiiwowiiwoooo

Everyone put their hands over their ears — but Old King Cole was the merriest man in the kingdom.

Jack and Jill

Jack and Jill went up the hill
To fetch a pail of water;
Jack fell down and broke his crown
And Jill came tumbling after.

Everyone said Jack was a good boy. He helped his mam fetch the water from the well at the top of the hill, and he helped her hang out the washing. He kept his toys tidy, and he was always clean and neat.

No one said Jill was a good girl. She was messy and untidy, and she left her toys all over the floor. When *she* helped her mam she spilt the water, and she trailed the washing in the mud. All the same, her mam and Jack loved her, and she loved them back.

One fine Wednesday, Great Grandma Brown came round to breakfast. Jack and Jill were playing hide and seek, and Great Grandma didn't see Jill hiding under the table.

'That boy Jack is a GOOD boy,' Great Grandma told Mam. 'He deserves a treat. The fair's coming to town on Saturday, so I'll take him. What's more, he shall have his very own sixpence to spend.'

'That's kind,' Mam said. 'But what about our Jill? She doesn't mean to be naughty.'

'HUMPH!' said Great Grandma. 'The day I see your Jill doing something right is the day I dance on my feathery hat. But fair's fair. If that day comes by Saturday I'll take her too. AND I'll give her sixpence. But you're not to tell her, mind!' Mam sighed. She didn't think Jill would ever do anything right by Saturday . . . but then she didn't know Jill was listening to every word.

When Great Grandma Brown had gone, Jill sat very still. She wanted to go to the fair. She wanted sixpence. But, most of all, she really REALLY wanted to see Great Grandma Brown dance on her feathery hat.

That night Jill tidied up ALL the toys. Her mam couldn't believe her eyes.

On Thursday Jill laid the table without being asked to. Her mam was so shocked she had to sit down.

On Friday Jill got up early and tiptoed downstairs. Jack heard her, and he followed her into the kitchen.

'What are you doing?' he asked.

'I'm going to fetch the water for Mam,' Jill said. 'I'm being good.'

'Why?' Jack asked.

Jill put her finger on her lips. 'Sssh! It's a secret! I'll tell you at the top of the hill!' Jack fetched the pail, and they hurried up the hill together. When they got to the top, Jack put the bucket down.

'Tell me the secret!' he said.

'If Great Grandma sees me doing something good,' Jill told him, 'she'll dance on her feathery hat! So, I'll keep on doing good things until she sees me!'

Bumpetty Bumpetty

Jack's eyes sparkled.

'Ha!' he shouted, and he jumped in the air – and fell over the bucket. Down the hill he rolled, BUMPETTY **BUMPETTY BUMP!**

Jill tried to stop him, but she fell too – BUMPETTY **BUMPETTY BUMP!**

'OUCH!' Jack wailed. 'My head!'

'Poor Jack,' Jill said. 'Let me rub it better.' And so she did – just as Great Grandma came stumping round the corner.

'What's going on?' she asked.

'Jill's making me better,' Jack said. 'I fell over.' Great Grandma Brown stared at Jill. Then she took off her great big feathery hat, and danced up and down until it was flat as a pancake.

'Jack and Jill,' she said, 'you'd better be ready first thing tomorrow. I'm taking you BOTH to the fair!'

Next day, when Jack and Jill came back from the fair, Jack was laughing . . . and covered in mud.

And Jill was laughing . . . and neat as a pin.

Bump!

Mary, Mary, Quite Contrary

Mary, Mary, quite contrary,
How does your garden grow?
With silver bells and cockle shells,
And pretty maids all in a row.

Mary Minnipeg was a mermaid. She lived at the bottom of the sea with her mum and her dad and a crab called James. In the cave next door lived Mary's aunt and her six girl cousins. Every girl cousin had beautiful long hair, big round eyes and a lovely smile. Mary had short hair, a turned-up nose and a fearsome frown. Mary thought the six girl cousins were silly. They thought she was grumpy.

Mary's mum liked lying on a rock and singing. Her dad liked diving through the waves and laughing. Mary and James didn't like singing OR laughing. They liked sitting in their cave playing Snap. When Mary won she said, 'Good!' When James won he clicked his claws. Neither of them ever smiled.

'Mary,' her mum said one day, 'why don't you come and sing with me?'

'No thank you,' Mary said.

'Come and dive through the waves with me,' said her dad. 'It'll be fun!'

'No thank you,' said Mary. 'I don't want fun.'

'Come and play Dressing Up and Being Beautiful,' said her six girl cousins.

'No thank you,' said Mary. 'I want to play Snap.' And Mary and James went on playing Snap, until one morning Mary woke up and found the cards scattered all over the floor. James was gone.

Her mum said she was very sorry about James, but now Mary could come and lie on a rock and sing. Mary said she didn't want to. Her dad said he was very sorry too, but now Mary could try diving through the waves. Mary said she didn't want to. Her mum and dad sighed. 'She's so contrary,' said her mum as they swam away.

Mary went to the cave next door.

'Does anyone want to play Snap?' she asked, frowning fiercely.

'No, no, no!' sang the cousins. 'But you can play with us! Today we're dressing up as princesses . . . look what we have in our treasure chest!' Mary looked. She saw heaps and heaps of pebbles and pearls and shells and shiny glass, and all kinds of other bits and pieces tumbled together.

'See?' said her oldest cousin. 'I'm sure you could be a princess if you dressed up!'

'Humph!' said Mary. 'I don't want to be a princess. I'm going to be a gardener instead. I shall make a garden for my best friend James so he'll come back and play Snap with me.' Mary scooped up two heaped handfuls from the treasure chest and hurried away.

The six girl cousins waved her goodbye, and went on dressing up in necklaces and bracelets and crowns. After a while the littlest one said, 'What does a garden look like?' Her older sisters had no idea, so the littlest one said, 'Can we go and see Mary's garden?' And the others sang,

'Oh, yes, yes, yes!'

They tiptoed on their tails to the door of their cave, and peeped out. 'OOOOOOOH!' they all said together. 'It's BEAUTIFUL!' And it was.

There were rows and rows of cockle shells and silver bells, and little bits of green shimmery glass. There were swirly patterns of polished pebbles, and floaty seaweed like an enchanted forest. Right in the middle were shimmery pearls carefully arranged to spell out PLEASE COME HOME JAMES. The six pretty mermaids stood in a row and stared.

'You are SO clever, Mary,' said the oldest. 'Will you show us how to make a garden?' Mary looked at them thoughtfully. 'I might,' she said, 'if you play Snap with me later.' The cousins all nodded. 'YES!' they said.

And for the very first time in her life Mary Minnipeg smiled . . . and James, who was hiding behind a rock because he was so very, very tired of playing Snap, clicked his claws happily, and came out to play in his garden.

51

Hickory, Dickory, Dock

Hickory, dickory, dock,
The mouse ran up the clock.
The clock struck one,
The mouse ran down,
Hickory, dickory, dock.

Squeak! Squeak! Squeak!
Martha Ninepence liked mice.
She liked them a lot.
Her mum hated them. She said
they were dirty. Her dad did too.
He said mice were messy.
That's why Martha never told
anyone there was a little grey
mouse living under the great big
grandfather clock in the hall.
  Martha was happy she had a
mouse as a friend. Her mum never
had time to play with her because
she was too busy washing things.

Her dad didn't have time to play with her because he was too busy working. Rosie, the girl next door, looked nice, but she'd only just moved in, and Martha was much too shy to speak to her. Martha would have been very bored indeed if it hadn't been for George.

Martha knew the little grey mouse's name was George because he had told her so. She also knew he LOVED cake, but he didn't ever get to eat more than a crumb because he had a mouse mother, two aunts, and five baby sisters who all liked cake too.

'Do they live under the grandfather clock with you?' Martha asked.

'I've never seen them.' George turned very pink. 'I don't live there,' he explained. 'I hide there when my mother tells me to tidy up our nest.'

Martha nodded. 'My mum's ALWAYS telling me to tidy up my room too,' she said.

One day Martha got an invitation to Rosie's birthday party. She was very excited. She lay on her tummy by the grandfather clock and whispered to George.

'I'm going to Rosie's party this afternoon! I've wanted to be friends with Rosie ever since she moved in, but I was too shy to talk to her!'

'Martha! WHATEVER are you doing?' It was her mum. 'Have you tidied your room yet?'

Martha jumped up. 'Is it time to go?'

'No,' Mum said. 'Not until you've had a bath and washed your hair.' Martha rushed upstairs. She ran into her room and flung her clothes on the floor. Then she dashed into the bathroom, and jumped into the bath. When she'd finished she skipped into her bedroom – and her mum followed her.

'MARTHA!' she said. 'LOOK at this mess! There'll be NO party for you until you've tidied up! You've got until the clock strikes one!'

Martha gave a little gasp. 'How long is that?' she asked.

'Ten minutes exactly,' Mum said, and she shut the door behind her.

Martha began to cry.

'Squeak! Squeak!' George darted out from under a cupboard. 'Don't cry,' he said. 'I'll help you!'

'But you're too small,' Martha wailed. 'I'll never get everything tidied away in ten minutes!'

George twirled his whiskers. 'I've got an idea,' he said. 'Didn't your mum say you had to tidy up before the clock struck one?'

Martha nodded.

'Then we'll stop the clock!' said George. 'You get busy. I'll see to the clock!'

Martha smiled. 'Thank you,' she whispered.

Martha folded her clothes and put them away. She tidied her toys into a box. Then she looked round. Her room had never ever been so tidy.

'MUM!' she called. 'MUM!' Her mother came up the stairs. 'Goodness me,' she said. 'That's wonderful!' Then she looked at her watch. 'But I did say it had to be tidy BEFORE one o'clock – '

'Boing!!!!!'

Downstairs the clock struck one. Martha's mum shook her head. 'My watch must be fast,' she said. 'Well done, Martha!'

'Hurrah!' shouted Martha, and as she ran next door to Rosie's party she called, 'THANK YOU, GEORGE! I'll bring back a BIG slice of cake, just for you!'

Squeak! Squeak! Squeak!

Pat-a-cake

Pat-a-cake, pat-a-cake, baker's man,
Bake me a cake as fast as you can;
Pat it and prick it, and mark it with B,
Put it in the oven for Baby and me.

Mr and Mrs Button's house was so tall and narrow that bits were always bursting out of it. Sometimes it was a saucepan that came whizzing through a window. WHIZZZZZZZZZZZZ!!! Sometimes it was a pair of boots.

WHEEEEEEEEEEEEEEEEEEEEEEEE!!!

Sometimes it was the cat, MEEEOWWWWWWW!!! Today it was the baby.

The postman caught the baby, and he took it back at once. Bertie Button opened the door. He was the oldest boy.

'Yours, I believe?' said the postman, and he handed him the baby.

'Oops,' said Bertie. 'Mum wondered where she'd gone.'

The postman peered at the baby. 'Good looking baby,' he said. 'How old is it?'

'She's one today,' Bertie said.

'Well I never!' The postman beamed. 'Happy Birthday – er – what's your name?'

'She doesn't talk yet,' Bertie said. 'She goes "Goo goo goo!"'

'Goo goo goo!' said the baby.

'But she does have a name?' the postman asked. Bertie went pink. 'Ma and Dad can't agree, so we just call her Baby,' he said.

'No name? Dear me!' The postman patted the baby's head. 'Hope you'll be having a nice big birthday cake!'

'GOO!' said the baby enthusiastically. 'GOO goo goo!' Bertie went even pinker.

'Ma's made three cakes today, and she's burnt them all, as usual.' The postman looked shocked.

'Well I NEVER!' he said, and he fished in his pocket. 'No name, and no cake. We can't have that! Here's a shiny shilling. You run along to the baker right now, and buy this young lady a cake!'

'OOHH!' said Bertie. 'Thank you!' He swung the baby onto his shoulders. 'Come on, Baby! We're off to the baker's to buy you a cake!'

The bakery was empty when Bertie arrived.

'Hello,' said the baker's man. 'Can I help you?'

'We'd like a cake, please,' said Bertie. 'A cake for Baby.'

'Be with you in a minute,' said the man, and he went off to the back of the shop. A little girl came running in the door. She looked at the baby sitting on Bertie's shoulders, and she smiled.

'What's your name?' she asked.

The baby looked at her, and smiled. 'CAKIE!' she said. The little girl clapped her hands. 'Katie? But that's MY name! I'm Katie too! Hello, Katie!'

Bertie's eyes were very wide. 'WOW,' he said. 'Baby spoke! That's her first ever word!' Just then the baker's man came back with a big box. 'Here's your cake,' he said to Bertie. 'And I've put a B on it for Baby!'

'Thank you,' said Bertie, and he turned to go.

The little girl called, 'Goodbye, Katie!' and the baby waved.

Bertie rushed through his front door.

'Ma!' he shouted. 'Ma! Baby's said her first word! And look what we've got!' He opened the box. Inside was a pink cake, with one pink candle and a big letter B.

'B for Baby!' said Bertie. 'Look, Baby!'

'WAAAAAAAA!'

The baby suddenly began to scream.

'CAKIE!'

'Sh, Baby,' said Mrs Button, and she cut a slice of cake. 'There! Happy Birthday, Baby!'

'WAAAAAAAAA!' yelled the baby, and threw her spoon on the floor. 'Cakie! Cakie! CAKIE!' All the Buttons stared at the baby.

'What's the matter with her?' asked Mr Button. Bertie scratched his ear. 'Actually,' he said, 'I think Baby's given herself a name.' He looked at his sister, who was still yelling. 'Hey! Are you Katie?' The baby stopped at once, and beamed.

'KATIE!' she said clearly. 'Katie cake!'

'But what about the B for Baby?' asked Mr Button. 'It's on the cake!'

'B for Button!' said Bertie. He leant over, and drew a K beside the B. 'Happy Birthday, Katie Button!'

And Katie Button gave her brother a big sticky kiss.

HUMPTY DUMPTY

Humpty Dumpty sat on a wall
Humpty Dumpty had a great fall
All the king's horses
And all the king's men
Couldn't put Humpty together again.

Charlie Apricot was the cook's new helper in the kitchen at the Royal Palace, and he was *very* excited. Cook had told him he could take breakfast to the little princess, and he'd *never* met a princess before. Come to that, he'd never met a cook before.

Cook was quite ordinary, except when she got angry. When she was fed up she threw plates all round the kitchen, CRASH!! CRASH!! CRASH!! Luckily, she only threw plates at walls, not at people, so Charlie didn't mind. And he soon became very good at mending the broken plates with the pot of glue Cook gave him.

Charlie couldn't wait to meet the princess, but when he did he was very disappointed. She was called Princess Daisy, but she looked exactly like any other little girl – apart from the crown. What's more, before Charlie had even said 'Hello,' Daisy was ordering him to play dolls with her, and he couldn't get away. He hoped and hoped Cook would call for him, but she didn't.

The next day, when Cook asked Charlie to take Princess Daisy her breakfast, he asked if he had to.

'Yes,' Cook said firmly.

Charlie sighed. 'But I don't like playing dolls.'

Play something else, then,'
Cook told him.

So when Princess Daisy
wanted to play dolls,
Charlie showed her how
to play Snakes and
Ladders. And hide and
seek. And football. By
the end of the week he
was good friends with the
princess . . . but he was
worried because it was her
birthday on Saturday, and he
didn't have a present for her.
He asked Cook what he
should do, but she said
she was MUCH too hot
and bothered about
Princess Daisy's birthday
party to think of anything
else. She gave Charlie a
pile of broken plates and
the queen's best teapot to
mend, and Charlie went
on worrying.

Princess Daisy's birthday arrived. The king and the queen gave
her a great big china egg doll, and she loved it. She called it Humpty
Dumpty, and she carried it with her all morning.

When it was time for her birthday parade Princess Daisy insisted
that Humpty Dumpty came with her to watch. Charlie was sitting on
the palace wall, and Princess Daisy climbed up beside him.

'Don't sit there, dear,' said the queen. 'Sit on your throne!'
But Princess Daisy stuck her lip out. 'I WANT to sit on the wall with
Charlie and Humpty Dumpty!' she said. The queen sighed and said,
'Very well, dear. It *is* your birthday.'

The king's horses and the king's men marched up and down, and
they blew their trumpets, and then –

B O O M ! ! ! !

They fired a huge gun in honour of Princess Daisy's birthday. The
princess jumped and Charlie jumped. The wall shook, and -

Humpty Dumpty fell off the wall and broke into pieces. CRASH!!!!!!!!!

Princess Daisy cried and cried. All the king's horses and all the
king's men came running up, but they couldn't help . . . and neither
could the king or the queen. Nobody could stop Daisy
crying . . . until Charlie had a BRILLIANT idea!
He dashed off to the palace, and soon came
running back with his pot of glue. He mended
Humpty Dumpty even better than he'd
mended the queen's teapot, and Daisy said
that was the best birthday present she could
ever have. She gave Charlie a HUGE hug.

When the king, the queen, all the king's horses and all the king's men and Princess Daisy sat down to Cook's special birthday tea, Princess Daisy asked Charlie to sit next to her.

'Dear Charlie,' she said, offering him the very first slice of cake, 'if I promise not to play dolls, will you be the Royal Best Friend?'
And Charlie said, 'Yes please!'

Baa Baa Black Sheep

Baa baa black sheep
Have you any wool?
Yes sir, yes sir,
Three bags full.
One for the master
One for the dame
And one for the little boy
Who lives down the lane.

icky MacMuffler lived in a very small cottage at the end of Muddle Lane. His daddy, Master MacMuffler, was a shepherd who kept his flock of sheep on the high green hills. Every summer he went away to find them and catch them and shear off their wool, but Micky didn't mind. His gran, Dame MacMuffler, looked after him, and she was a wonderful teller of stories. She was also a champion knitter, and every year she won first prize at the County Fair for her scarves and her mittens and her hats and her blankets.

In fact, Dame MacMuffler was so busy knitting that she never had time to cook. She never had time to clean. She never dug the garden, or picked up sticks for the fire. She never painted the walls, or knocked in a nail. She sat in her chair all day and every day, telling Micky stories, and knit-knit-knitting.

Luckily Micky could cook. And clean. And he was good at finding sticks for the fire and growing potatoes, so they were very happy together until one day when the North-East wind blew and blew and BLEW. By the end of the morning the very small cottage had begun to creak.

WHEEEEEEEEEEEEEEEEEEEE!!!

blew the wind.
By lunchtime it was groaning.

WHOOOOOOOOOOOOOOOOO!!!

blew the wind.
Just before teatime the roof blew off.

WHEEEEEEEOOOOOOOEEEEEEEEOOOOOOOEEEEEEEE!!!

blew the wind.

Micky stood staring with his mouth wide open. Dame MacMuffler sat calmly in her chair, knit-knit-knitting.

'Micky dear,' she said. 'Run up into the hills and fetch your daddy home from shearing, there's a good boy. We can't live in a house with no roof. If it comes on to rain my knitting needles will get rusty, and I'll never make another pair of mittens or win another prize.'

So Micky ran down the lane and up into the hills, the wind whirling round and round and round him.

He found a hill full of white sheep with thick white woolly fleeces, but he didn't find his daddy.

He found a hill full of spotted sheep with long spotted fleeces, but his daddy wasn't there either.

He found a hill full of black sheep with neat clipped coats, and a heap of sacks stuffed with thick black wool – but he STILL couldn't find his daddy.

The sun sank low into the clouds, and the sky grew dark. Micky sat down amongst the sacks of wool, and blew his nose hard. He was trying not to cry.

'BAAA!' said a voice. 'BAAA! You're the master's son, aren't you? What's the matter with you?'

Micky rubbed his eyes. A big black sheep was standing right beside him.

'I can't find my daddy!' said Micky. 'The roof's blown off our house and Gran says that if it rains her knitting needles will go all rusty, and she'll never be able to win a prize again! Oh, PLEASE can you help?'

'Baa,' said the sheep, and she looked up into the sky. 'It's a fine night tonight,' she said. 'And my toe bones tell me it'll be a fine day tomorrow. That should be time enough.'

'Time enough for what?' asked Micky.

'Time enough for Dame MacMuffler to save the day!' said the sheep.

'Choose three bags of wool, and take them home: one for you, one for the master, and one for the dame. There's JUST enough time for a champion knitter like your gran to knit you a brand new roof.'

'Thank you VERY much,' said Micky, and he chose the three biggest bags.

'Now,' said the sheep, 'you run along home, and I'll find the master for you.'

'THANK YOU!' said Micky. He hugged the sheep, and picked up the bags of wool. Then he ran and ran until he was home.

'GRAN!' he said as he burst through the door. 'I've enough wool here for you to knit us a new roof!'

'Oh, Micky!' said Dame MacMuffler, 'what a clever boy you are!'

All night long she knitted, KNIT KNIT KNIT, KNIT KNIT KNIT. . . and all the next day . . . and by evening the cottage had a brand new black woolly roof. It kept the cottage so warm that Micky had to open all the windows. As he opened the very last window he looked out, and there was his daddy walking home, with a black sheep close beside him . . . just as the rain began.

Georgie Porgie

Georgie Porgie, pudding and pie,
Kissed the girls and made them cry;
When the boys came out to play,
Georgie Porgie ran away.

Georgie Porgie was a naughty little pigling. He crept into the larder, and he ate a big potato pudding. Then he ate an enormous apple pie. Mother Pig was very cross indeed when she found him licking the pie dish.

'You're a BAD little pig!' she told him. 'Go and play outside!'

83

Lucy the Lamb and Clara the Calf were skipping in the yard with Georgie Porgie's six little sisters.

'I'll twirl the rope,' Georgie said, but he twirled it too fast.

'Go away, Georgie Porgie,' said Clara. 'You're spoiling our game!'

'Skipping's silly,' Georgie said. 'Let's play Kiss Chase!' And he rushed towards his littlest sister Peggy shouting, 'Kiss! Kiss! Kiss!' Peggy squealed loudly, and ran away as fast as she could go. Georgie ran after her, and grabbed her by her little curly tail.

'Caught you!' he shouted, and gave her a kiss. Peggy began to cry, and Georgie ran towards Lucy.

'Your turn!' he called, but when he kissed Lucy she began to cry as well.

'Go AWAY, Georgie!' Clara said crossly. 'You're spoiling EVERYTHING!'

'Can't catch me!' yelled Georgie, and he scrambled up to the top of the haystack.

'Ha ha ha, hee hee hee – I'm on a haystack and you can't catch me!'

Clara, Lucy and the six little pigling sisters stared up at him.

'You're mean, Georgie Porgie,' said Lucy. 'I'm going to tell my big brother Larry!'

'And I'M going to tell my big brother Carlo!' said Clara.

'Hey diddle dumpling, see if you dare! I'm on a haystack and I don't care!' sang naughty Georgie Porgie, and he danced up and down and threw hay at them.

'Baaa!' bleated Lucy, and she trotted off to find Larry.

'Mooo!' mooed Clara, and she hurried off to find Carlo.

Peggy and her five little sisters scurried away home.

Georgie Porgie danced on top of the haystack . . . until he saw Larry and Carlo stamping into the yard, looking VERY angry.

'Oops!' said Georgie, and he buried himself in the hay.

'Come down, Georgie Porgie!' baa-ed Larry.

'Come and play with US, Georgie Porgie!' bellowed Carlo.
Georgie Porgie said nothing at all. He stayed as still as could be on the top of the haystack. Larry and Carlo looked at each other.

'Shall we play football here in the yard?' asked Larry, and he winked. Carlo winked back. 'Good idea,' he said.

Larry and Carlo played a LONG game of football. Georgie Porgie waited for them to go away . . . but they didn't.

When they'd finished playing football they played Long Jump. And then they played High Jump. And then they played football again.

Georgie Porgie began to feel VERY hungry.

At last Lucy came to call Larry home for his supper. Clara came with Lucy, and she told Carlo his supper was ready too. Nobody came to tell Georgie Porgie that HIS supper was ready. As soon as Carlo and Larry had gone he slid down the haystack and ran away home.

'Mother, Mother, Mother!' he squealed as he dashed through the door. 'I'm STARVING!'

'But Peggy told me you were playing with the boys,' said Mother Pig. 'She said you weren't hungry!'

'But I AM!' wailed Georgie.

'Oh dearie me,' Mother Pig said, 'and we've eaten nearly ALL the rhubarb ice cream!' She looked at the six little girl piglings. 'Shall we let Georgie have the last helping?'

'NO!' said Peggy, and then she giggled. 'Well – not unless he lets US chase HIM round the yard tomorrow!'

TWINKLE, TWINKLE, LITTLE STAR

Twinkle, twinkle, little star,
How I wonder what you are!
Up above the world so high,
Like a diamond in the sky.

The sun was slowly sinking behind the purple western hills, and behind the evening clouds the stars were getting ready to slip into the dark blue sky.

'Tonight,' said a large and glittering star, 'my brothers and I will shine over the ships at sea. The sailors will look out for us, and steer their ships safely home.'

'Tonight,' said a star who was as bright as a new pin, 'my family and I will light up the soft dark velvet of the southern skies. Men and women will be dazzled, and many will fall in love.'

'Tonight,' said a gleaming star with a thousand silver sisters, 'we will spangle the heavens with our beauty. Travellers will stop and wonder at us, and go on their way refreshed by our presence.'

A little star heard what the others were saying, and he snuggled close beside his mother.

'How important they are,' he said. 'I could never be as grand as they are.'

'They think far too much of themselves,' his mother said, sniffing. 'Every star is there to sparkle for someone. They just want to make a song and dance about it, and show off.'

89

'I'd like to sparkle for the children,' said the little star, sighing, 'but by the time we come out they're tucked up in bed. I try and see in through their windows, but they're listening to their mummies and daddies reading them a story, and they don't see me. Or else they're already fast asleep. I try and twinkle in their dreams, but it's not at all the same. I do wish I could shine a little earlier . . . just as the sun goes down.'

'What's that? What's that? A little star who's not happy?' It was the moon, and she was looking most surprised. The little star's mother blushed. 'I'm so sorry, my lady,' she said. 'He doesn't know what he's saying.'

'Yes I do!' said the little star eagerly. 'I do, I do! I want to watch over Little Miss Muffet as her mother calls her to come inside! I want to be shining high in the sky when Jack and Jill peep out of their window just one last time before they go to sleep! And . . .' the little star gave a huge sigh, 'then they'd all know I'd be there if they woke from a bad dream, and they'd smile before snuggling deep down into their pillows.'

'A little star who's not happy?'

The moon looked thoughtful. 'I suppose it could be allowed,' she said. 'I'm very fond of children myself . . . but wouldn't you be lonely, up in the sky all on your own?'

'Oh, NO!' exclaimed the little star. 'I'd be so happy . . . and besides, by the time the children were sleeping, all my brothers and sisters and cousins would be sparkling all around me!'

The moon smiled at the eager little star. 'Very well, then,' she said. 'So be it! Come with me, and we'll go up into the sky together!'

The little star blew his mother a kiss, and then floated up and up into the velvet evening sky behind the silver moon. And he twinkled and twinkled as he'd never done before. Far below on earth the children saw him, and smiled and waved at their very own star.

And if you look up into the evening sky, just as the sun has set, you'll see that little star twinkling all on his own . . .

. . . just for you.